Ellen Stoll Walsh

Pip's Magic

Harcourt Brace & Company
San Diego   New York   London

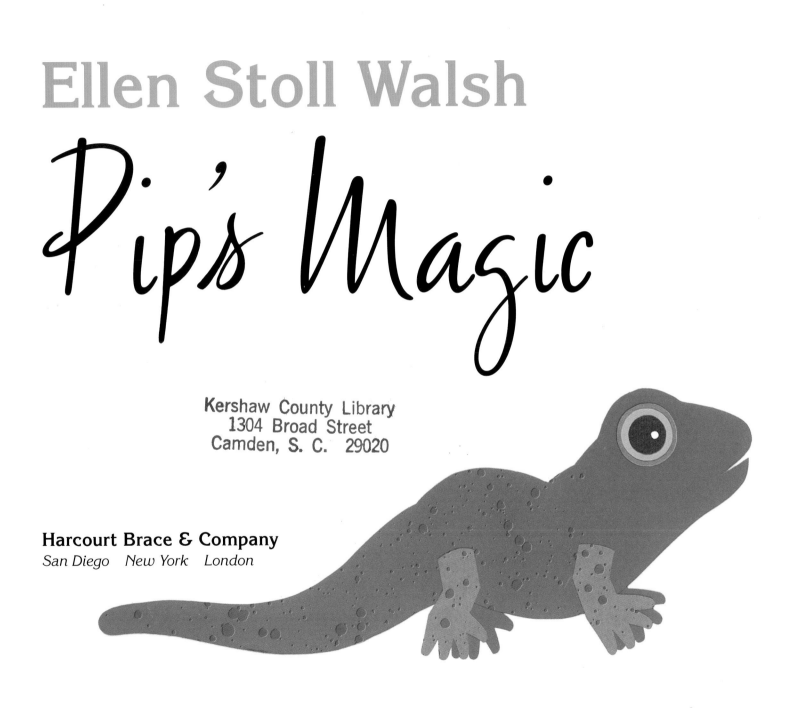

Requests for permission to make copies of any part of
the work should be mailed to: Permissions Department,
Harcourt Brace & Company, 6277 Sea Harbor Drive,
Orlando, Florida 32887-6777.

Library of Congress Cataloging-in-Publication Data
Walsh, Ellen Stoll.
Pip's Magic/Ellen Stoll Walsh.—1st ed.
p.   cm.
Summary: Pip the salamander is afraid of the dark,
so he sets out in search of a wizard who will help him
overcome his fear and unexpectedly finds courage.
ISBN 0-15-292850-2
[1. Fear of the dark—Fiction.   2. Salamander—Fiction.
3. Animals—Fiction.]   I. Title.
PZ7.W1675Pi   1994
[E]—dc20   93-34155

First edition   A B C D E

Printed in Singapore

The illustrations in this book are cut-paper collage.

The display type and text type were set in Korinna by

Harcourt Brace & Company Photocomposition Center, San Diego, California.

Color separations were made by Bright Arts, Ltd., Singapore.

Printed and bound by Tien Wah Press, Singapore

Production supervision by Warren Wallerstein and Kent MacElwee

Designed by Camilla Filancia

For Robin Pulver, Elizabeth Wild,

and Molly Hunter Giles

"I'm afraid of the dark," said Pip. "Even shadows scare me."
His friends didn't know how to help.

But the frogs did.

"Ask Old Abra, the wizard," they said. "He's over by the big pink rock, turning stones into mushrooms."

"Magic, of course!" shouted Pip. "Magic might help me be brave in the dark. I'll find Old Abra and ask him for help."

Pip ran to the big pink rock.

"If you are looking for Old Abra, you're too late," said a mouse.

"He went into the woods, and he won't be back."

Pip sighed. "It's as black as shadows under a rock in there. But the wizard has magic, and I need magic to be brave in the dark. I must try to catch up." And he followed Old Abra into the woods.

"No one could find the wizard in here," said Pip. "I can't find my own feet."

At last he saw sunlight peeping through the branches, and he followed it out of the woods.

"If you are looking for Old Abra, you're too late," said a sparrow. "He went into the tunnel and he won't be back."

"Then I'll go, too," said Pip. "Oh, dear. The tunnel is as black as night with my eyes closed. But the wizard has magic, and magic might help me be brave in the dark." And he followed after Old Abra.

Pip ran up and down the tunnel and looked in all the darkest
hiding places. The wizard wasn't there.

Pip found his way out just as night was falling.

"If you are looking for Old Abra, you're too late," said a snake.

"He went over those hills, and he won't be back."

"The night is as black as river mud," Pip said with a sigh. "But I need magic to be brave in the dark." And he climbed through the night after Old Abra.

Pip found Old Abra resting where the sun rises.

"Please give me magic, Old Abra. I need magic to be brave in the dark," said Pip.

"But you already have magic," said the wizard. "You found it in the woods and in the tunnel and in the night. You have enough, and maybe some left over."

Pip tested his magic just to be sure.

Old Abra was right. He wasn't afraid of the dark.

Pip took his leftover magic to a quiet place.

"What are you doing?" asked a frog.

"*Shh,*" said Pip. "I'm going to turn stones into mushrooms."